Mr. Nogginbody Gets a Hammer

David Shannon

Norton Young Readers

An Imprint of W. W. Norton & Company
Independent Publishers Since 1923

For Bonnie and Blue

For information about permission to reproduce selections from this book, write to Permissions, W. W. Norton & Company, Inc., 500 Fifth Avenue, New York, NY 10110
For information about special discounts for bulk purchases, please contact W. W. Norton Special Sales at specialsales@wwnorton.com or 800-233-4830

Library of Congress Cataloging-in-Publication Data
Names: Shannon, David, 1959– author, illustrator.
Title: Mr. Nogginbody gets a hammer / David Shannon.
Description: First edition. | New York, NY : Norton Young Readers, an imprint of W. W. Norton & Company, [2019] | Summary: After buying
a hammer to fix a loose floorboard, Mr. Nogginbody learns a lot about home repairs—and what is, and is not, a nail.
Identifiers: LCCN 2019001976 | ISBN 9781324003441 (hardcover)
Subjects: | CYAC: Dwellings—Maintenance and repair—Fiction. | Repairing—Fiction. | Hammers—Fiction. | Humorous stories.
Classification: LCC PZ7.S52865 Mr 2019 | DDC [E]—dc23 LC record available at https://lccn.loc.gov/2019001976

W. W. Norton & Company, Inc., 500 Fifth Avenue, New York, N.Y. 10110
www.wwnorton.com

W. W. Norton & Company Ltd., 15 Carlisle Street, London W1D 3BS

1 2 3 4 5 6 7 8 9 0

I'm Mr. Nogginbody.
I love to slide in my socks!

Ouch! what was that?

"Dan's Hardware Store helps you help your home!"

"That was a nail.
You need a hammer."

Okay, here goes!

Why on earth did it do that?

Easy does it.

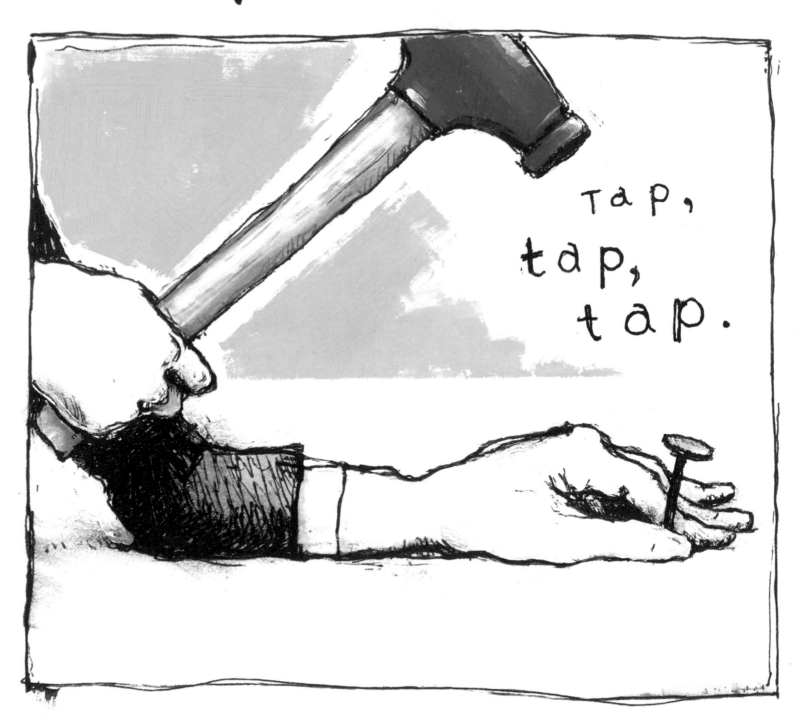

tap, tap, tap.

I

fixed

it!

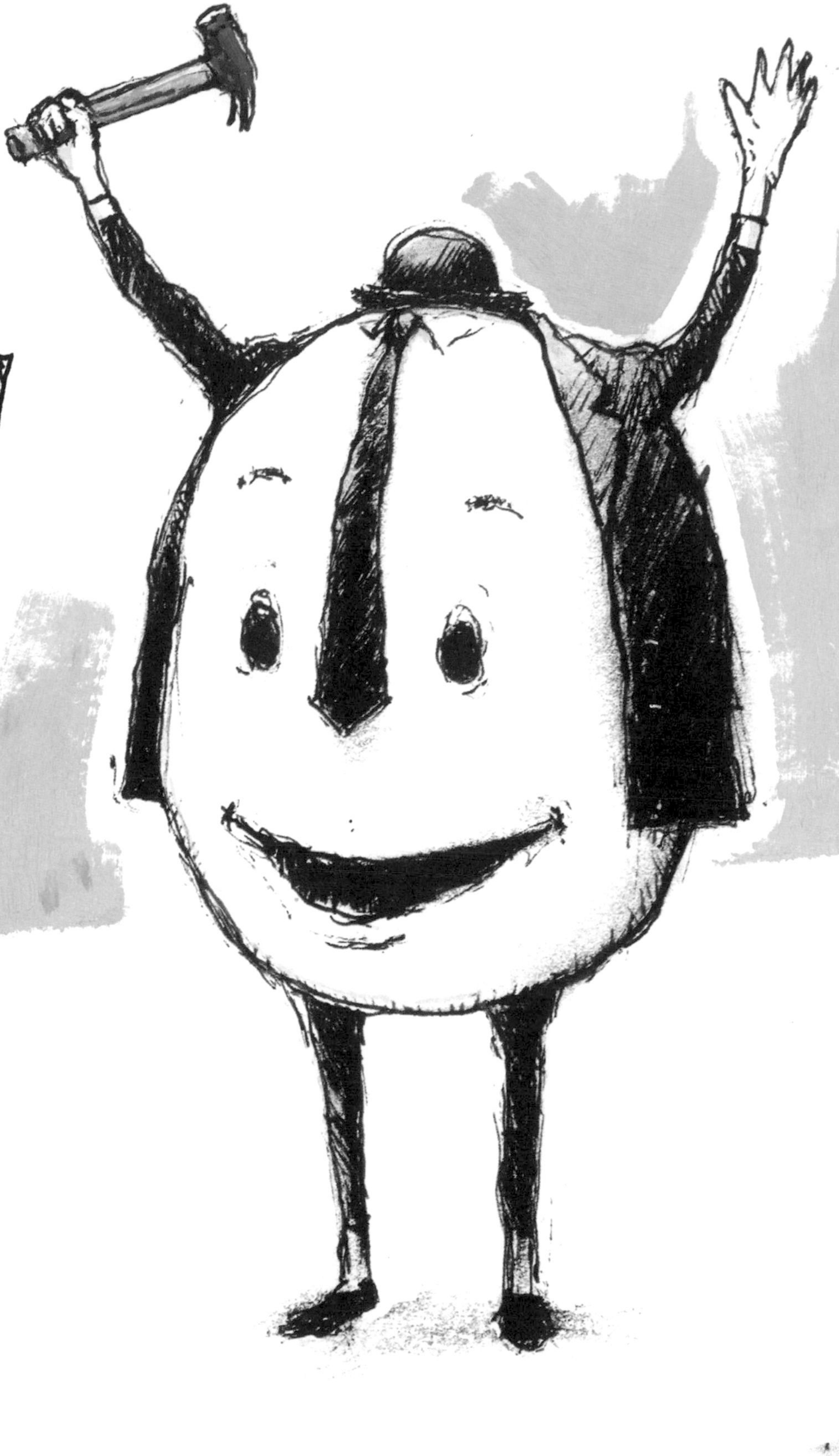

Here's another one!

Oops! I botched it.

Hey, I bet that's what this end is for.

Who knew it would be so easy?

Hey, that picture is crooked.

Fixed it!

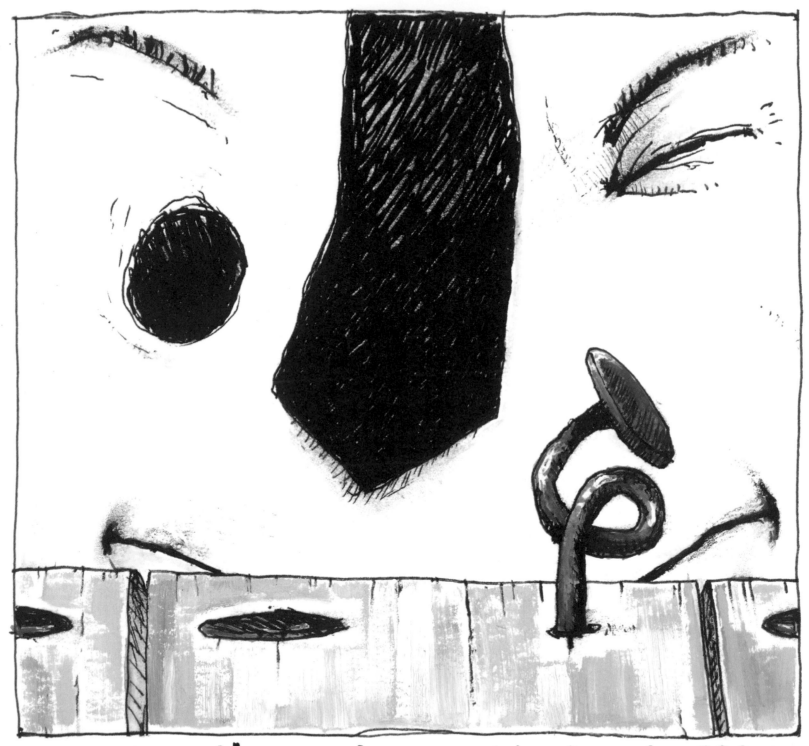

Hmm... that doesn't look like a nail.

But this does!

Fixed it!

Fixed

That's the same kind of nail as in the bathroom!

Oopf! Missed it!